FOR SNORRI
x

Text and illustrations © 2016 by Morag Hood
First published in the UK in 2016 by Two Hoots, an imprint of Pan Macmillan,
a division of Macmillan Publishers International Ltd.
Published in the United States in 2017 by Houghton Mifflin Harcourt

www.hmhco.com

The text type was set in Catalina Typewriter.
The display type was set in Arco Web.

Library of Congress Cataloging-in-Publication Data is available.
ISBN 978-0-544-86842-7

Manufactured in China
10 9 8 7 6 5 4 3 2 1
4500606612

Carrot & Pea

Morag Hood

Houghton Mifflin Harcourt

Boston   New York

This is Lee.

He is a pea.

All of his friends are peas.

Except Colin.

Colin is not a pea.

He is much too tall

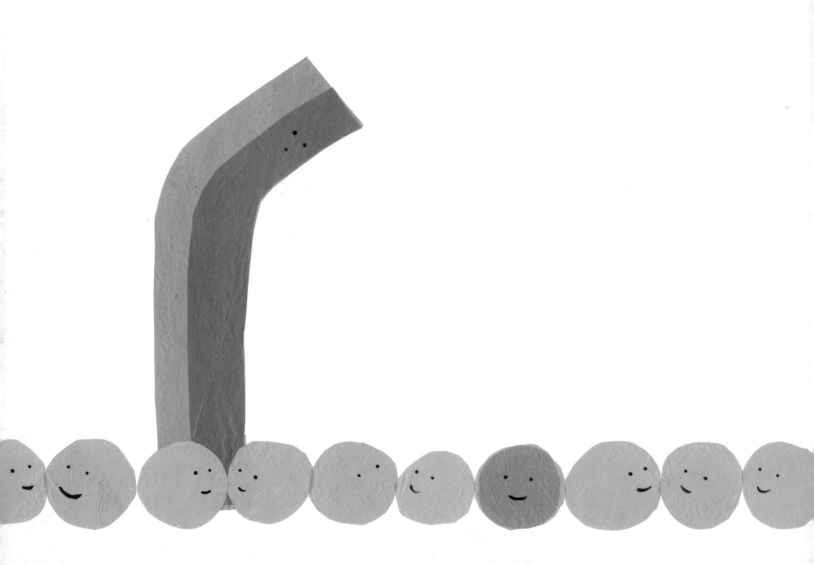

and much too orange.

He can't roll

or bounce,

and he isn't very good
at hide-and-seek.

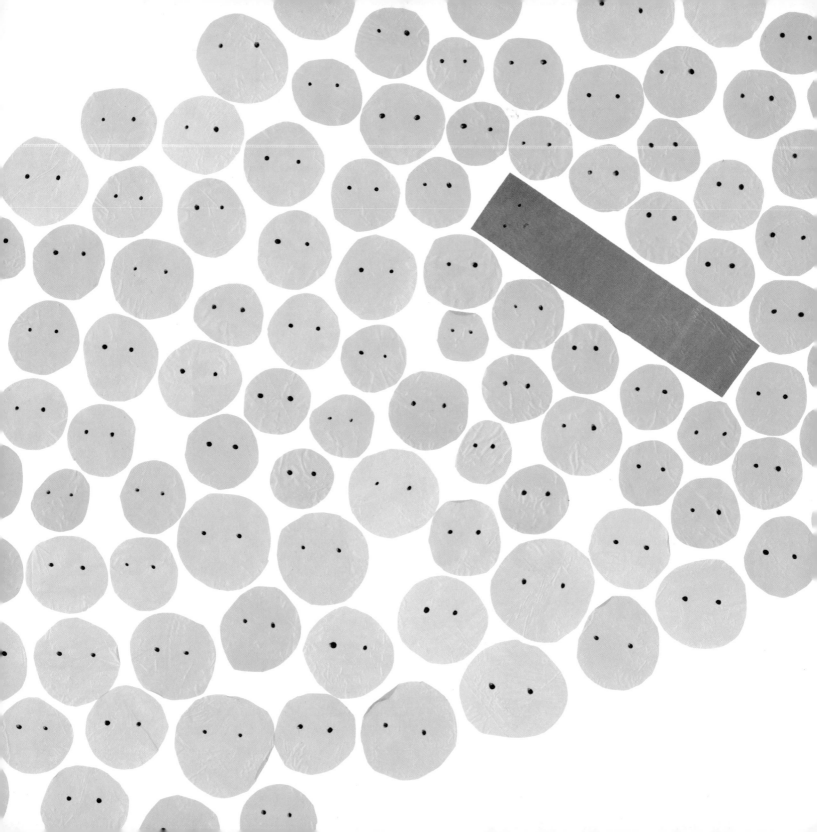

But Colin is an
excellent tower,

a fantastic bridge,

and a great slide.

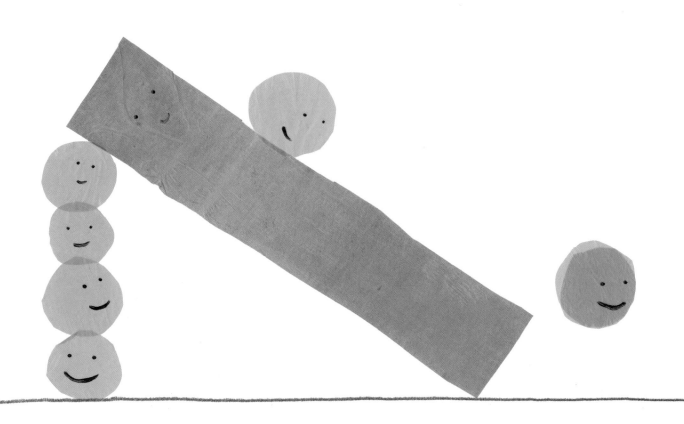

Colin isn't at all like Lee
and the other peas.

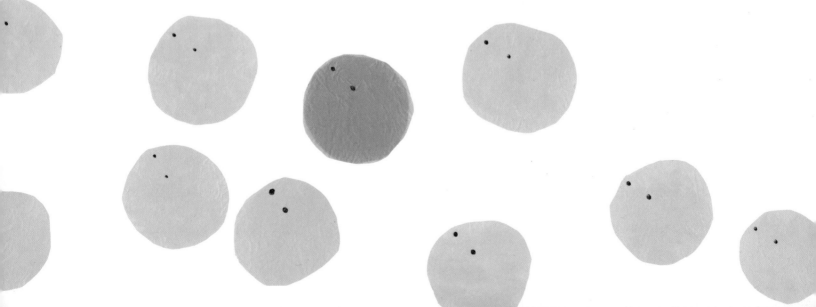

And that's just the
way they like it.